Sid is Sick

Written by Emma Lynch
Illustrated by Jess Mikhail

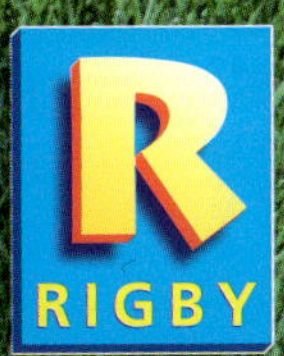

Viv is a vet.

Sid's job is to help.

I am the vet, Sid.
Help me fix Fox.

Swop jobs, Viv.
Can I be the vet?

No Sid, I am the vet ...

Just help me fix Pup.

Swop jobs, Viv.
Let me be the vet.

No Sid. Duck is sick.
I will help Duck.

11

Just help me jab Cat.
I am the vet.

PILLS

Fix me, Viv.
I am sick.

I am sick
of the vet!